To Robyn - Easter 1986

Love, Uncle Leroy and Aunt Sue

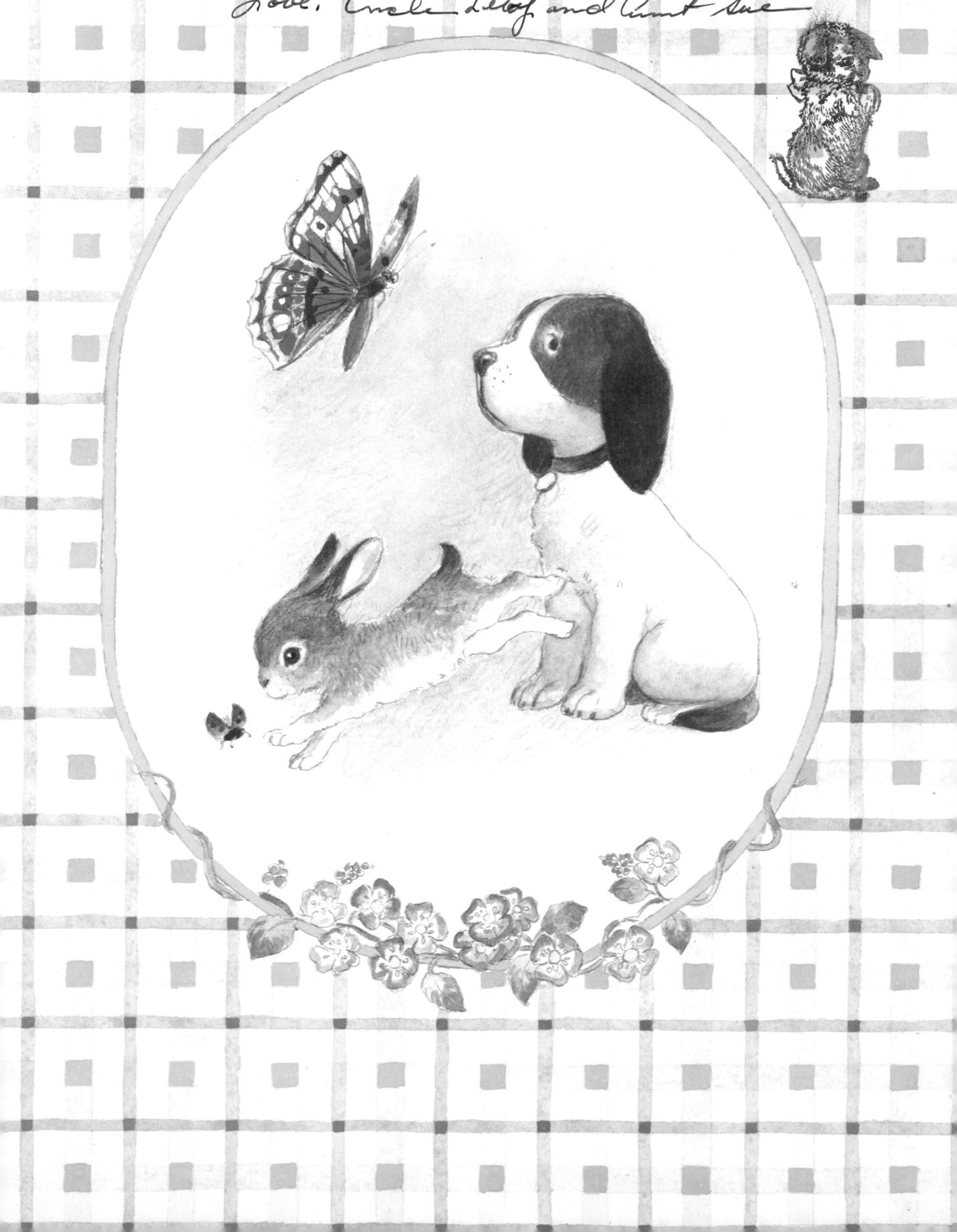

JULIE
and the pony

Illustrations by José-Luis Macias S.
Original story by J. Barnabé Dauvister
Retold by Jane Carruth

Woof! Woof! Woof! What's the matter, Muffin? Why are you barking so loudly? Oh! There's a pony in our garden.

Hey! Stop it, little pony! Mummy's roses are far too pretty to be eaten like that. You must not spoil the lovely flowers which make our garden so beautiful.

Look Muffin! Look at the pony now! He is standing on his hind legs. I think he is saying that he is sorry.

You are a smart little pony. You are really very clever. Have you escaped from the circus? If you want to, you can play with us until they come looking for you.

Come on everybody! We're going to have a picnic on the grass. Gee up, little pony. My doll, Miss Flora, wants to trot.

There's nothing like being outside in the sunshine to make you hungry. Muffin and the squirrels are hungry too and want something to eat.

Ponies have huge appetites! The apples on the apple tree are
fun to eat. "Bad pony! These apples do not belong to us!"
Julie scolds.

The little pony is so hungry that when Julie wants to share out her cake, he picks it up and eats it in one mouthful. "Goodbye cake!" thinks Muffin miserably.

There is worse to follow! As soon as they are home, the greedy pony snatches the tablecloth with his teeth so he can pull the apples toward him. Crash! Everything falls on the floor.

Oh dear! What a naughty trick that was!

Muffin, do be careful. You're going to knock the fish bowl over! What an upset there has been today!

Wow! I've saved the fish!
Poor Muffin! You're soaked.

Just look what you've done, you silly little pony! If you hadn't been so greedy none of this would have happened! What a mess! It's time you went back to the circus!

Julie's naughty guest has gone back to the circus and it's peaceful again. What a busy day it has been. Julie and Muffin won't easily forget their friend, the pony!

Published in the United States and simultaneously in Canada by Joshua Morris, Inc.
431 Post Road East, Westport, CT 06880
Printed in Belgium